THE
GIANT

BARE KNUCKLE

THE GIANT

JONATHAN MARY-TODD

darbycreek

MINNEAPOLIS

Text copyright © 2014 by Lerner Publishing Group, Inc.

Darby Creek
A division of Lerner Publishing Group, Inc.
241 First Avenue North
Minneapolis, MN 55401 U.S.A.

Website address: www.lernerbooks.com

Cover and interior photographs © iStockphoto.com/Steve Krumenaker (brick background); © iStockphoto.com/tomograf (paper texture); © iStockphoto.com/ Abomb Industries Design (woodrat); © iStockphoto.com/ankur patil (fist).

Main body text set in Janson Text LT Std 12/17.
Typeface provided by Linotype AG.

Library of Congress Cataloging-in-Publication Data

Mary-Todd, Jonathan.
        The giant / by Jonathan Mary-Todd.
            pages   cm. — (Bareknuckle)
        Summary: In 1874 Manhattan, Luc, sixteen, at nearly seven feet tall and seemingly impervious to pain, has become a local boxing star but when kangaroos are introduced to the ring, Luc's tender heart leads him to run away to save a joey.
        ISBN 978–1–4677–1457–0 (lib. bdg. : alk. paper)
        ISBN 978–1–4677–2411–1 (eBook)
        [1. Boxing—Fiction. 2. Kangaroos—Fiction. 3. Self-reliance— Fiction. 4. Size—Fiction. 5. Circus—Fiction. 6. New York (N.Y.)— History—1865–1898—Fiction.] I. Title.
    PZ7.M36872Gi 2014
    [Fic]—dc23   2013020526

Manufactured in the United States of America
1 – SB – 12/31/13

TO BROS OF ALL SPECIES

CHAPTER ONE

Luc let the thin man hit his face two times, then a third blow. The man would tire himself out this way. The sharp, familiar taste of blood filled Luc's mouth.

The other man was shorter and thick around the waist. His fists couldn't quite reach Luc's face, so he hit Luc low, jabbing beneath Luc's ribs.

"Come on now, Luc!" Mr. Chilton shouted. "Enough games, let them have it!"

Luc held a fist out, keeping the two fighters at arm's length. The shorter man swatted at the air. The fight's enforcer, Oakley, stalked the edge of the circle, keeping clear of the fighters inside.

Mr. Chilton shouted again, leaning over the painted line. "You've put the fear in them, Luc! Let's hurry up."

Oakley turned to face Mr. Chilton, and Chilton stepped away.

The thin man swung at Luc again, a right cross, same as before. Luc batted the man's hand away and drove a fist between his eyes.

As the thin man sunk to the floor, his partner moved toward Luc, shuffling right and left. Luc heard Oakley start the ten count for the first man.

Luc had to reach down to hit the short man, and his swing was clumsy. The short man tipped his head, sinking it into Luc's white belly. Luc let the man strike him again and then grabbed the man's shoulders, lifting him off his small feet and throwing him to the floor.

Once Oakley had finished the second ten count, Mr. Chilton ran to pat Luc's back.

"The Boy Giant of the North, gentlemen!" Chilton said. "The strength of two men is no match for his might!"

Chilton walked from the circle toward the bar, and Luc walked behind him. The Woodrat Club's owner, Mr. Mayflower, raised a glass to them.

"A fine fight, Lew, wouldn't you agree?" Mr. Chilton said.

"Fine enough," Mayflower said. A man on a stool slid Mayflower a coin, and Mayflower refilled his mug.

Chilton bent against the bar. "And if I may be vulgar enough to raise the matter of tonight's prize . . ."

"We'll put it toward your tab," Mayflower said. He spat in a spit bucket by his feet.

"Of course, Lew. Good. Very good."

Mr. Mayflower turned away and reached into a coin jar. He set a coin in Chilton's hand, moving his eyes to Luc. "For the boy. You see he gets something to eat. We want him here next week. Maybe a fight with the Irishman next time."

———————

"Unsavory sorts, those two men tonight. Most unpleasant," Mr. Chilton said, moving his lower lip over his moustache. "Very unsavory. As if two men against one weren't a favorable situation! If that Oakley looks the other way on a headbutt one more time, I'll have half a mind to intervene myself!"

Chilton took another bite from the loaf of soda bread and broke off a piece for Luc. When he turned, he was surprised to see that Luc was two heads back. The streets of the Bowery were often crowded, and Luc had a hard time walking through.

Luc took bread and started to chew it, but his mouth was still raw from the fight. He pulled the chunk in two. One part would sit in his mouth until it softened. The other part Luc would save for the birds.

"These men are jealous, Luc. That's all," Chilton said. "It's only a matter of time until you and I are the kings of Manhattan! You'll see. No more living in that flophouse. When I found you, I knew. This was a golden opportunity for both of us."

Mr. Chilton had found Luc splitting logs in Quebec. That was in 1870, Chilton said. Luc had been twelve or thirteen, his best guesses. Four years later, Luc's English was better, but he still spoke just a few words at a time. With Mr. Chilton, Luc often could simply nod and keep silent. Mr. Chilton was a confident man and showed his education when he talked. In any case, Luc liked the excuse to keep quiet.

Mr. Chilton sounded frustrated when he spoke about the flophouse. Mrs. Maxwell, the owner, would get upset when Chilton called it a flophouse at all. Soon they'd live someplace more refined, Mr. Chilton would say. But Luc liked the place. He had his own room there, and Luc had not had that before. The bed was too short for him to lie on all the way, but if he moved the bed frame sideways he could hang his feet off of the end.

Sometimes Mrs. Maxwell's daughter Molly would bring ice from the kitchen for Luc's face, but not that night. She wasn't in her quarters down the hall.

Luc smiled when he looked in the oval mirror next to his sink. His bruises reminded him of a peeled potato, but bruises would always go away.

Luc did not like to fight very much. It bothered him to think about the men who hadn't won—he wondered what they thought about when they looked in the mirrors next to their sinks. But he liked to see Mr. Chilton happy. And it was rare to find your way to something you were truly good at, Mr. Chilton said. Luc agreed that this was true.

After Luc had rinsed his mouth out, he remembered the rest of the bread. He took it from his pocket and crumbled it carefully along the windowsill.

Mr. Chilton had asked once why the windowsill was so white with bird droppings. Chilton would have thought it was silly to save food for birds to eat. So Luc had said he didn't know.

No birds came to the windowsill before Luc went to bed, but it was already nightfall. Luc would see them the next morning. He licked his thumb and snuffed out a candle, smudging the wax with his thick fingers.

CHAPTER TWO

The Irishman Killpatrick was not taller than Luc, but he was a very tall man. He stood nearly six and a half feet tall, even taller than Oakley.

Mr. Chilton began cheering as Oakley rang the bell, spilling suds onto the floor from his mug.

Killpatrick moved fast for a big man. Faster than Luc. He struck Luc twice in the kidney and then danced backward, wiping strands of red hair from his forehead.

"Focus now, Luc!" Mr. Chilton shouted. "Confidence!"

Killpatrick swung again, into the center of Luc's chest. The wind left Luc, but he leaned forward with a right hook, catching the Irishman in the jaw. Killpatrick was tall enough to hit without crouching.

Luc tried to grab Killpatrick and lift him, but Killpatrick cursed and wriggled in Luc's arms. Too early. The two fighters tumbled outside the circle and into a table nearby. Mugs shattered, covering the sticky ground with a new layer of beer.

Oakley ordered the drunks nearby to clear a path and then shoved himself between Luc and Killpatrick, yelling up at them to get back to where the fights were held. Luc went first, not turning his back on the Irishman. His heart thundered like cannon fire.

Killpatrick ducked left and came up quick, jabbing Luc above his doughy cheek. Luc groaned again and brought a hand to his face. Killpatrick had drawn blood. Luc raised his fists and stepped closer to the Irishman, then doubled back. The man held broken glass between his knuckles.

Luc looked to Oakley but couldn't find the words to speak. Killpatrick stayed close. He moved Luc around the circle with a series of feints. Luc tried to look not at the pointed glass but at Killpatrick's shoulders, his feet, to see how the man would move next. The Irishman flailed, trying for a haymaker. Luc caught his fist with both hands and began to squeeze.

Luc wanted to let go when he heard the first pop but he knew that he could not. Even when Oakley began to yell and pull at Luc's wrists, Luc held on. Even when he heard the glass crack. Only when Luc saw Killpatrick's eyes close did he know he could stop.

Oakley pointed for Luc to leave the circle as Mr. Chilton hopped the line and slid between them.

"Disqualified, Chilton," Oakley said.

"Now, now, now—just look at the boy," Chilton said. "Clearly this is nothing more than a misunderstanding. Certainly, next time, now that Luc is very clear that we do not finish our matches this way, I agree that—"

"No prize, Chilton. And I'm prepared to toss you and the boy out of here."

Mr. Chilton pointed to the shards of glass by accident, waving for Oakley to listen. They lay in Killpatrick's mangled palm. Oakley shook his head, rang the bell, and raised Luc's hand.

At the bar, Chilton let an arm fall gently against the counter and opened his own palm.

"If you would be so kind, Lew," he said.

Lew Mayflower took a stack of bills and split it in two. "Half for you, half for your tab. You're a lucky idiot, Chilton."

"Thank you, Lew," Chilton said flatly. He turned to Luc. "And well done, of course, Luc. As I say, focus is key. A vigilant eye. You could've cost yourself the match, there, when you let that brute grab the glass, but you regained your focus . . ."

Luc felt sad and tired. Embarrassed too.

A murmur came to him from across the club. Many men's voices at once.

"My word," Chilton said. "Luc, I believe we're about to see something extraordinary."

A man in a maroon suit wheeled a cart through the crowd. An animal stood on top.

"Oakley!" Mayflower shouted. "The creature's here. If this gets messy, you get it out of the building."

"There will be no need for that, I assure you," the man said. He left the cage by the fighters' circle, then stepped to the bar and took a bow. "H. Thomas Hardt. You must be Mr. Mayflower."

Mayflower nodded. "The arrangement's the same as I said in the letter. You wanna let that thing fight? Fine. The house gets fifty percent."

"Very well," Hardt said. He turned to face the Woodrat Club. The men's eyes were already on him. "Gentlemen! My name is H. Thomas Hardt. And I am about to present you with a very rare opportunity. Direct from that cage, from across the ocean, is the cunning, the dangerous, the kangaroo of South Australia!"

A couple of the men clapped, and Hardt waved them silent.

"Who will test his mettle against this creature? Only a modest fee is required. Knock it out and you'll double your money. But if Genghis knocks you outside the ring, well,"— Hardt laughed—"you won't have been the first, my friends!"

"Marvelous!" Mr. Chilton whispered to Luc. "Really, marvelous!"

Luc watched Mr. Hardt's trainer unwrap the kangaroo's binds as a few men lined up outside the circle. The trainer could not have been much taller than his animal. He wore a faded cowhide vest, with what looked like scars or burns or both crawling out from underneath it, all across the man's skin. The kangaroo twitched and looked in every direction in the club's dim light.

As the first Woodrat man entered the circle, the kangaroo bounded toward him before Oakley could ring the bell. It struck the man twice with its arms as the bell clanged and booted him, stumbling, outside the border before the clanging stopped.

The kangaroo did the same to the next man, and then the next, until Oakley stopped using the bell. Luc looked away anytime one of the men swung his fist. He wanted to go home. But as the kangaroo's trainer put its binds on again, Mr. Chilton thrust a glove out to the man in the maroon suit.

"Mr. Hardt? Randall Chilton," he said. "And what an honor it is to make your acquaintance."

CHAPTER THREE

Luc held himself still as the cleaning boy, Silas, stitched closed the wound on Luc's cheek. Silas had been mopping up spilled beer and broken glass, and his arms were tired. Both boys had to be careful.

Mr. Hardt and Mr. Chilton clinked mugs at the table behind Luc. Hardt's trainer had taken the kangaroo away, and Mr. Chilton had many questions about the man.

"Ian?" Mr. Hardt said. "Hah! He's something

of a grotesque, I know. All those years wrangling wild beasts. Got himself all chewed up. But he's excellent help! Keeps those creatures in line . . ."

Silas pulled the needle away from Luc and snipped off the rest of the thread. Before Luc could say thank you, Hardt snapped his fingers at the boy. "Another round, young man!"

"You heard him, Silas!" Mr. Chilton said, his face flushed. "Hurry now!" He turned back to Mr. Hardt. "And you, my good man—how did you come to own such a remarkable creature?"

"I'm what you might call a globetrotter," Mr. Hardt said. He tugged at a stained maroon lapel. "This silk—you see it? Direct from the Orient!"

Mr. Chilton nodded many times. "Yes, yes, very fine. Very fine indeed." He prodded Luc's shoulder. "Do you see the man's jacket, Luc? The Orient!"

Luc nodded.

"My trade is the exotic," Hardt said, grabbing the next round from Silas's tray. "For a time, it was imports. All kinds. Then, during a visit to the Australian outback, I met Ian and his animals. And I told Ian, 'My friend, we have a fortune waiting for us . . .'"

"A kangaroo," Chilton said, shaking his head. "I can still scarcely believe it."

"Ah-ha! Kangaroos," Hardt replied. "Come, let me show you something."

The two men stood up, then grabbed the backs of their chairs for balance. Luc caught Mr. Chilton's empty mug as it tumbled from the table.

———————

Mr. Chilton was shocked to hear that Mr. Hardt and his trainer were also staying at the Maxwell flophouse.

"But really!" Chilton said. "A man of your refinement! It's—Luc and I won't be here long either, you see. Only temporary. But a fellow like you—"

"One of the burdens of being a man of the world," Hardt said. "Most of my assets are tied up elsewhere."

Mr. Chilton nodded thoughtfully and then began to hiccup.

Hardt clapped his hands together as they reached the outside of the flophouse. "Here we are!"

He led Luc and Mr. Chilton around back, where Ian the trainer was sharpening a large blade against a smooth black rock. Ian nodded to Hardt but said nothing. Behind him were two cages—one for the kangaroo Luc had seen earlier, another for an animal one-third its size. Luc thought it might be a rabbit at first. When he looked closer, he saw that it was another kangaroo.

"We used to bring the mother along, too," Hardt said. "Drove costs up, but it helped keep Genghis settled. The other one passed away at our last stop, regrettably. Even Ian's not sure why."

He rapped his knuckles on the bars of the adult kangaroo's cage.

"Genghis has been agitated ever since. Not that it hurts him in the ring, mind you. And his mate was kind enough to give us this young one before she fell ill. They keep the young inside a pouch, did you know? It's bizarre. The joey left the pouch only a couple weeks before the mother died. Looks to be a future prizefighter himself, if I may say so."

Luc squatted down before the joey's cage. He met the kangaroo's black eyes for a moment and smiled. As he began to poke a finger through the bars, a sudden clanging drove him back and sent the joey to the far side of its pen. Genghis rattled against the walls of the cage next door.

"Luc!" Mr. Chilton barked. "Behave yourself."

Luc slunk backward. The trainer, Ian, stopped sharpening his knife and fixed on Luc with a glare.

"Sorry about that, Tommy," Chilton said to Mr. Hardt.

"No matter, no matter," Hardt said. "Ian, if Genghis acts up like that again, make sure he gets a good prodding, understand?"

Ian nodded and began sharpening his knife again.

Luc stayed far away from the kangaroo cages. He sat down against a couple of crates stacked in the alley behind the flophouse and began to drift in and out of sleep.

Mr. Chilton and Mr. Hardt continued to talk. Mr. Hardt had ideas far beyond his kangaroos, he said, and all he needed was the money of a few bold investors. They would all be wealthy men down the line. Chilton was honored by the offer, and he was sure that with a little time he would be able to find the funds somewhere. It shouldn't be a problem. Ian said very little, but Luc continued to hear the *scrrrtch* of his knife against the rock throughout the first hours of the morning.

CHAPTER FOUR

Mrs. Maxwell's daughter Molly smiled shyly as she set down biscuits for Luc and Mr. Chilton, then turned pale when she saw Luc's new stitches. Luc put his head down and began to eat.

In the seat next to Luc, Mr. Chilton squinted and tried to peer inside the spout of the coffeepot. As he lifted the pot for another cup, the coffee poured slowly, like mud. Chilton rubbed one of his temples with his free hand.

"This . . . wretched . . . sludge," he said.

"Mrs. Maxwell seeks me dead, Luc. I'm sure of it now. What else explains this vile brew? I'll open this pot to find a rodent carcass, you'll see! That woman . . . I come to breakfast expecting sweet relief, and what do I find? My stomach, under attack!"

"You're welcome to make your own coffee, Mr. Chilton," Mrs. Maxwell said, clearing the empty biscuit tray and leaving the table with another round of sausages.

"Hah! You'd like that, I'm sure," Chilton said. "To pay you for room, board, and breakfast, then do half the work ourselves. I'll leave the coffee making to you, Edna, thank you very much. Randall Chilton's dollar goes as far as it can, not a hair shorter."

"About that dollar . . ."

"Very soon! Coming very soon. On that you have my word. A change of fortunes is coming our way, Mrs. Maxwell, you'll see! Big things coming for me and the boy."

"I'll be overjoyed, I'm sure," Mrs. Maxwell said. "You and he have until the nineteenth for your rent."

"Of course, of course."

Once Mrs. Maxwell returned to the kitchen, Mr. Chilton cut into a sausage and continued to tell Luc about the ache in his head.

"Too much of a good thing, Luc. Heed these words. It can be quite dangerous indeed."

Through a mouthful of sausage, he asked Luc if Luc would mind lending a hand.

"I'm serious about our change in fortunes," Chilton said as Luc kneaded the back of his neck. "I can see it from here. This Mr. Hardt— I hope you were giving him your full attention last night. He's a man with much wisdom to share. Take it from one who knows."

A stream of grease dribbled down his chin. "Imagine, Luc. You and that animal sharing a bill all down the mid-Atlantic! Or this chance to invest Hardt mentioned . . ." He tapped the butt of his fork against the table. "That? That's the knock of opportunity, my boy."

When Mr. Chilton's head felt better, Luc excused himself from breakfast. He wrapped the last sausage in a cloth napkin as he left, in case any dogs were outside. Some days, Mr. Chilton would take him around, and they would try to find odd jobs for a person of Luc's size to do. But that day, Mr. Chilton said he felt too tired to do anything. Luc stepped outside the flophouse and walked toward Fourteenth Street. He left a trail of sausage for the dogs of the Bowery along the way.

Union Square was crowded that afternoon. Luc let some men on horses pass and then crossed into the park. Usually children ran around the statue in the center, but that day most of them stood huddled in one place. Luc peered over their heads to see three men in strange clothes and white makeup.

One of the men juggled a set of balls in the air. Another held a stick up to his face and then spat out fire. The children around him gasped and jumped back. The third man held his hands out as if he were caught inside a small room.

Luc didn't like watching the third man. He tried to watch the juggler, but his thoughts turned to Mr. Hardt's kangaroos.

Luc wasn't happy when he had to fight, but Mr. Chilton was right. It was something he was good at. And Quebec was worse than Manhattan. It was colder, and Luc had worked all day there, and the other men there had not been as friendly as Mr. Chilton.

Genghis seemed good at fighting too. And maybe Australia had been a worse place for Genghis and the smaller kangaroo. Luc couldn't say for sure. He didn't know anything about Australia.

What happened to Genghis if he lost a fight? Luc didn't know the answer to that either. He had never lost a fight himself, although he was sure Mr. Chilton would be angry if he did. And Mr. Hardt seemed a lot like Mr. Chilton. Luc was glad Mr. Chilton didn't keep a friend like Ian the trainer around.

Parents of the children watching the men in white makeup had formed a second ring around the performers. Some of them looked at Luc with worry.

On the way back to the flophouse, Luc saw that the sausage bits were gone, but he also saw a man in a butcher's smock chasing dogs away as two other men carried cuts of meat into his shop. The dogs must have still been hungry.

Before Luc went back to his room, he walked around the back of Mrs. Maxwell's, checking to see if Ian was around. Ian was not.

Luc stepped slowly toward the kangaroo cages. He told himself that he could only stay for a minute—he knew the trainer would stop by the cages again soon. But he did not stay even that long. As Luc approached, he woke up Genghis, who had been sleeping at the back of his cage. The kangaroo rattled at his bar again, sending Luc running down the street.

CHAPTER FIVE

Luc's fight with Boston John had been faster than his fight with Killpatrick the week before. First fight of the night. Afterward, Chilton complained to Oakley that Luc was an earner, a big earner, but half the usuals at the Wood-rat weren't likely to show up for another hour, and that he was beginning to have real concerns about the way these nights were booked.

Luc looked around for a stool that would support him, then brought it to a table in one of the club's small corners. He'd have to move the table to get out again, but this way, fewer men would spill their drinks or poke him with their elbows on their way to the bar.

From his out-of-the-way spot, Luc didn't hear the squeal of the kangaroo cart until Ian dragged Genghis inside. Mr. Hardt followed him and took his hat off to the few men who dotted the club floor.

"Thomas!" Mr. Chilton called out.

"Good evening, my friend, good evening!" Hardt replied. He walked past the fighter's circle, toward Lew Mayflower at the bar. "Mr. Mayflower. Has talk of Genghis's debut last week whet your boxers' appetites? Any takers tonight?"

"The Irishman," Mayflower said. "Killpatrick."

Luc hadn't noticed Killpatrick come in either. He sat in another corner, cloaked in shadow.

In the past week, men at the Woodrat had been whispering about Killpatrick—that losing to Luc had made him feel small, had made a cruel man crueler. At the mention of his name, he left his seat and marched toward Mr. Hardt and Mr. Mayflower. He stopped only to leave an empty mug on the counter and then continued to the circle. He struck the air once, twice, then yanked the towel off his neck. It landed a few feet from Luc's table.

"Looks like he's ready, Hardt," Mayflower said.

Mr. Chilton clapped his hands. "Ooh, what a bout this is!"

Hardt motioned for Ian to prepare the kangaroo.

The fighters stood at opposite sides of the circle, Genghis jittering wildly, as Oakley rang the bell. Luc gripped the tabletop until his fingers began to warp the damp wood.

The Irishman ground his knuckles in his palm, and the kangaroo hopped toward him. The animal jabbed its paws forward, but the hits didn't land, and Killpatrick was too wide, too tall to hold in place. It tried again, insistent, and the hits did not connect. Outside the circle, Mr. Hardt clenched the handle of the animal's cart.

The first time Killpatrick swung, he caught Genghis on the side of his snout. The kangaroo hopped to the side with a yelp. Killpatrick bared his teeth, grinning.

After the first punch, Luc had stopped watching. He stared at the wrinkles in the table instead, listening to the shuffling of the fighters' feet. And then he felt Killpatrick's eyes on him. At least that's how he would remember it. The Irishman glared at him and turned back to the animal, driving a left cross into its neck.

The kangaroo fell to the floor. It gurgled through the ten count. Oakley rang the bell again.

Luc rose up, bumping the tabletop, and Mr. Chilton rushed over to demand that he stay put. Ian and Mr. Hardt dragged the limp animal toward its cage, Hardt leaving a trail of threats and curses.

———

"That Irish barbarian!" Mr. Chilton shouted, a few steps behind Mr. Hardt and Ian the trainer. "A character like that should be barred from the

Woodrat! I think I'll take it up with Mr. Mayflower myself, in fact . . ."

Luc stepped behind Mr. Chilton, peeking over the man's head to see the kangaroo cart that Hardt and Ian were wheeling down the avenue.

They stopped when they reached the back of the flophouse, Mr. Hardt and Mr. Chilton both panting. Mr. Hardt had lost his hat along the way, and he patted his head absently. Luc stayed back, waiting for the red to leave the men's faces.

"My livelihood! Gone!" Hardt said. He kicked one of the bars of the joey's cage. "What is Mayflower going to do about that?"

Mr. Chilton raised a finger as if to speak but then stayed quiet.

"All of my plans . . ." Hardt continued. He scanned the building next to the cages, then turned to Chilton, speaking in a lower voice. "This Mrs. Maxwell . . . is she very strict about late payments?"

Chilton shook his head.

"Well, there's that at least," Hardt said. "A moment to regroup."

Luc watched as Ian ran his hand along Genghis's neck. The kangaroo's moan had settled into something like a pained, steady purr.

Hardt called over to him, "Well, all right, out with it, Ian. I don't suppose there's any chance it'll fight again?"

Ian told him there was not.

"I suppose we'll have to do the honorable thing then, yes? Put old Genghis out of his misery?"

Ian agreed. Luc put a hand to his face as Ian unsheathed his blade.

"Not in front of me, Ian! I don't want to see it!" Hardt said. He pointed to Luc and Mr. Chilton. "Good lord, we're among people . . . Though do see that it's done soon. The dogs'll be out in force tomorrow if we don't get the thing away from here . . ."

Ian began to pull Genghis's cart away, down the street and into the black of early morning. As Mr. Hardt and Mr. Chilton began to talk further about ways to avoid Mrs. Maxwell, Luc slunk toward the cage that held the smaller kangaroo. This one didn't clatter at its bars—just looked back at Luc as he looked in. Luc wanted to say something to it about the other animal, but wasn't sure, in French or English, if he'd be understood.

To Luc's surprise, Mr. Hardt stepped next to him, although he continued speaking to Chilton: "The little one's got real potential, I think. A scrapper in the making. What with Genghis gone now, I'll have to talk to Ian about how soon until it can start to train."

CHAPTER SIX

Luc had spilled coffee over his hands at breakfast and could not eat his biscuits. As Molly arrived to mop up the mess, Luc retreated to his quarters. The coffee he'd been able to drink stirred uneasily in his stomach.

Mr. Chilton had left early that morning, complaining of bad sleep and explaining to Luc that if any creditors came around, Luc should tell them Mr. Chilton had moved to a different address. Luc had not seen Mr. Hardt or Ian at breakfast. He had been glad of that, at least.

Luc's room felt smaller than usual as he walked back and forth across the wood floor. Occasionally he would stop at the one window and stick his head through, but the men and women outside would not hold Luc's attention.

One day in Quebec, when Luc was chopping wood, a few of the others dragged a man into camp. The man had been hunting for furs when snow began to fall, covering some of the traps he'd set. Soon the man stepped into one of them. The older men brought him indoors before he could bleed out, but it took five of them together to pry the trap loose.

Genghis's fight the night before worked like a trap on Luc. Each thought of it was painful, but he could not shake the memory. He had felt the drain throughout the morning, and he felt it in his room.

Luc didn't know how fast a joey grew. Neither did Mr. Hardt, he remembered. If Luc knew how to read, he would have tried to read about it. If the younger kangaroo were to box someday, Luc knew it would meet another man like Killpatrick.

Luc did not think the joey should have to fight. One kangaroo was enough. One was too many, Luc thought.

Luc had fed dogs and birds for a long time now, and he believed he could care for a joey. Mr. Chilton might not even be angry if Luc waited long enough to tell him. Mr. Hardt traveled the world, and he was likely to leave again sometime. Luc could tell Mr. Chilton after that. He closed the door to his room and started down the stairs, taking them one step at a time.

Luc looked down at the animal like he had the night before. Once again, the kangaroo looked back. Luc wondered if it recognized him. The kangaroo's black eyes wouldn't say.

Luc yanked once at the cage's lock, and the kangaroo scampered backward at the clang. The alley was empty, but Luc still began to worry. He could break the lock with time, though not without a lot of noise.

Luc started to sweat, glancing down the alleyway again.

Maybe he could try another way. He wedged his fingers between two bars and pulled each bar away from the other. He wasn't sure afterward if the bars had moved or not. He tried again and his hands began to throb. The bars had started to leave imprints in his palms, and maybe later there'd be bruises.

On the third try, Luc heard the cage's metal groan—not from where he pulled, but near the crossbar at the top. At the joints where the bars met the ceiling of the cage, rust covered the iron like ivy.

Luc could reach the top without stretching. He grabbed two of the bars in each large hand, pressed a boot against the cage, and pulled.

The kangaroo flinched at Luc's deep grunts, and Luc slowed his breaths, failing to stay quiet. With a ping, two bars came loose, then two more. Luc laid them on the ground and crouched down to see the joey.

The animal took a few hops in Luc's direction, then backed away. Luc set his throbbing palms on the floor of the cage. It approached him once more, sniffing the hands, testing him. Luc let it be for a moment. When the kangaroo came even closer, Luc grabbed it up, unprepared for the flailing. He tucked the animal underneath his shirt as it scratched at his belly and tried to push off. He held the kangaroo against his chest until it settled. Then he stumbled, damp with sweat, out of the alley.

CHAPTER SEVEN

The kangaroo thumped its tail whenever Luc came too close. It had already bitten at his fingers when he put it down in the corner. Luc wondered if Mrs. Maxwell would be upset about the scratches on the floor and thought about moving his bed to hide them.

Maybe the animal was scared by the sudden change, Luc thought. A lot had happened in the last few weeks. He sat down in the room's opposite corner and just watched it for a while.

Once Luc had gone long enough without approaching the kangaroo, it began to look at him less anxiously, as if he were a large tree in the middle of a plain. Something unusual, but no cause for concern.

Sometime after the sun had signaled midday, the animal let loose some droppings near the foot of Luc's sink. Luc had not thought about this. He knew he would have to clean up the mess but he decided he didn't have to yet.

The kangaroo settled in a cool spot on the floor, away from the light of the window, and began to lick at its forearms. Luc felt thirsty. The joey might be thirsty too. Luc held his eyes on the animal to make sure it wouldn't follow him out, then stepped into the hallway and closed his door.

Mrs. Maxwell's kitchen was empty when Luc peeked inside. He found a dish for water and some stale biscuits on the counter. Did a kangaroo eat biscuits? Luc thought it would.

He began to feel tired as he moved back up the stairs—he got like this with no breakfast—

and balancing the dish and the biscuit tray made his hands throb again. He tucked his head before the low hallway ceiling. When he looked up again, Mr. Chilton was standing by the door to his room.

"Afternoon, my boy! Feeling peckish, I see."

Luc shrugged, trying to keep the biscuits on the tray.

Mr. Chilton reached for a biscuit, then winced after his first bite and put it back. "Any of those debt collectors stop by while I was out?"

Luc told him no.

"That's a relief, anyway," Chilton said. "Perhaps they've moved on, bigger fish. It's only right—we're hard-working people after all, just trying for a good day's ... Is something the matter, Luc?"

As Luc shook his head, he and Chilton heard a thump from underneath the doorway.

"What on earth was that?" Chilton asked.

Luc shrugged again.

"Do you have anything to tell me, Luc?"

The two of them heard another thump. Mr.

Chilton moved a pair of fingers down the length of his moustache. "Open that door, Luc."

Luc shook his head.

"Open it."

Luc turned the handle slowly. Mr. Chilton began patting himself down with a handkerchief.

"Now you've done it," Chilton said. "You've really done it."

Luc kept the dish and biscuits in hand and refused to meet Chilton's eyes.

"What are we going to do about this, Luc? Mr. Hardt will be furious. Small chance he'll agree to a partnership now. This was an opportunity . . . ! Oh, I'm feeling faint."

Chilton forced himself within Luc's line of sight. "What did you think, you oaf? That you could keep it?"

Luc's eyes pleaded for that very thing. In the corner, the joey continued to lick at its wrists.

Chilton sighed. "Now, I suppose if Mr. Hardt were to never, never discover what has happened to his kangaroo, there's no way he could hold us accountable . . ."

Luc looked to Mr. Chilton and smiled. Chilton set a hand on Luc's shirtsleeve.

"But you have to keep that creature right here. Do you understand, Luc? No taking it outside, no playing about. If word gets to Thomas, we're both in a lot of trouble. Do you see?"

Luc nodded yes.

"Good," said Chilton. "Very good. I'm counting on you now to be discreet."

Chilton gave the kangaroo a final glance, put his handkerchief away, and stepped back toward the door. As he started to leave, he whispered, "You keep the animal right here, Luc. Do you promise?"

Luc promised.

Once Mr. Chilton had gone to his quarters, Luc set down the water dish and the tray of biscuits. When the kangaroo didn't come near, Luc began to crumble a couple of biscuits in his hand. He sat on the ground and nudged himself toward the joey. As he got closer, he opened up his palm.

At the sight of food, the joey inched its way

to Luc, tramping across the floor on all fours instead of hopping. It reached Luc's palm and sniffed around, then nuzzled its small snout into his hand.

When it had eaten all of the crumbs, Luc crumbled another few biscuits. The kangaroo lapped up water in the meantime. They did this until every biscuit was gone.

As late afternoon drew near, Luc's stomach settled, but he still felt very tired. He put a towel over his window's curtain bar to block out the sun. Rather than lie on his bed, he sat back on the floor, a few feet from the joey, and leaned against the wall.

"Dors bien, mon ami," he said—Sleep well, my friend.

With the towel across his window, Luc wasn't sure how long he'd slept for. A quarter of an hour or well into the evening? He woke with a start to stiff banging on his door.

Light from the hallway soon filled the room as Mr. Hardt shoved his way inside. Mr. Chilton followed, several steps behind Hardt, manically dabbing the sweat on his brow.

"I'm here for what's mine," Hardt said. "Get up. Grab the animal. And come with me."

CHAPTER EIGHT

Mr. Chilton spoke to Luc in a warm, bouncy tone that said nothing was the matter. He also continued to sweat, spouting out droplets until his handkerchief was useless.

"First thing, Luc, is to not get upset," Chilton said. "I'm sure you feel that I've misled you, and I can see why. But sometimes one has to make difficult choices, you see, for the benefit of all."

Luc turned away as Chilton stepped closer.

"I've spoken to Mr. Hardt, and he's been very understanding about this whole ordeal," Chilton continued. "He's a man of the world, remember. I'm sure he's made a few rash decisions in his time!"

Chilton chuckled at that and looked to Hardt, who did not return the laugh.

"We're very lucky, Luc," Chilton said. "He's willing to turn the other cheek. But you must cooperate now. It's his animal, after all. His business! I'm sure you can appreciate . . . If you want something of your own, we can see about that. Perhaps we'll tether one of those dogs . . ."

"Enough, Chilton," Mr. Hardt said. "Is your boy going to give me the kangaroo?"

Mr. Chilton nudged Luc as Luc faced the corner, both of their eyes on the joey.

"Go on, Luc," Chilton said. "Let's help the man."

The animal had woken when Luc did, when Hardt had thrust open the door. It stirred in its spot on the floor, eyes wide to capture the hallway light. Luc thought of a bear trap snapping shut.

"Up, up! Mr. Hardt is being very patient, Luc."

Luc scooped the kangaroo into his arms. It did not bite or scratch him like before.

"There we are, there we are," Mr. Chilton said.

Luc stood up with the joey, but he couldn't meet Mr. Chilton's eyes. Chilton asked him if he had anything to say to Mr. Hardt, and Luc did not.

"Well, all's well that ends well. That's what I say," Chilton said.

"There's also the matter of the damaged cage," Mr. Hardt replied.

"Not to worry, Thomas, not to worry," Chilton said. "That will come out of Luc's earnings, of course. Which I suspect are on the rise. This is all to our shared benefit, really. Think of it: The Boy Who Can Bend Iron. Mr. Mayflower will be asking for Luc at the Woodrat seven nights a week, soon enough!"

As Luc stepped into the hall, following Hardt and Chilton, his tall shadow blocked the light that had carried over into his room. He looked back once into the dark, and Mr. Chilton scolded him to keep moving.

"Now, Thomas, about the matter we discussed earlier," Chilton said. "Your search for investors. I do hope you won't hold this against us. It's only a hiccup, I'm sure, on the path to a fruitful partnership . . ."

The men's voices filled the hallway, but they drifted past Luc. Other things seemed louder: the creaking of the boards under his boots, an occasional murmur from the joey. Luc lowered his head and followed Hardt and Chilton down the flophouse stairs. The heat had lasted into the early evening.

He followed the men through Mrs. Maxwell's room for hanging laundry, toward the building's side exit. Mr. Chilton cringed as he peeked through the side door's small, square window.

"Oh dear," Chilton said. "She looks like a savage on the warpath today."

"Who?" said Hardt.

A moment later, Mrs. Maxwell entered through the back and halted at the sight of the two men in tattered suits.

"Misters Hardt and Chilton! They very men I've been hoping to see. Would you happen to have the money for your lodgings? It's past due for the both of you. But you know that."

Mr. Chilton cleared his throat. "Well, Edna, I believe Mr. Hardt and I are in similar positions in that—"

"In that he's a heel, and you're the muck that's stuck on it. Where is my money, you swindling—"

Mrs. Maxwell's mouth fell open as she glanced beyond Hardt and Chilton to the back of the room, where Luc cradled the kangaroo.

"Mr. Hardt!" she said. "When I told you I'd let you lodge with those things—and I had a mind to point you somewhere down the street—we agreed they'd stay outdoors! Outdoors! Oh, the filth I'm sure you've tracked in here already! I charge a fair rate, I said, and I don't expect any trouble—"

"Boy," Mr. Hardt muttered. "Take the creature to the cage."

Luc made his way to the side door and then out into the street. When Mr. Hardt and Mr.

Chilton attempted to follow, Mrs. Maxwell grabbed them by the collars. Luc couldn't make out what she said once she slammed the side door shut behind him.

He stepped quickly around the corner toward the cages, adding to the time he would have away from Hardt and Chilton.

Mr. Chilton got angry sometimes, Luc thought, but he had never lied before.

Had Mr. Chilton lied before?

"Luc!" Chilton's voice rounded the corner from back by the side entrance. "Where are you, son?"

The street that stored the cages was empty of people. Luc's strides widened and then broke into a sprint. He huffed past the iron pens and onto another block completely, still holding the animal against his chest.

CHAPTER NINE

Luc had outrun the voices of Hardt and Chilton very quickly, but he continued to look over his shoulder. He stumbled out into the mess of Lafayette Street, trying to squeeze between the crowds of people as heads turned beneath the whimpering joey.

For a moment, a few loose dogs ran to follow Luc and the kangaroo, then turned to chase a loose chicken. The many busy people of the Bowery filled Luc's path, slowing his escape to a walk. Trudging along a series of storefronts, Luc knocked a barber pole off its hinges with a stray elbow. Calling out an apology behind him, he bobbed into another alleyway. A bed-sheet, hanging between windowsills, caught him across the face.

When Luc peeled off the sheet, he saw Ian the trainer in front of him.

Luc wrapped the cloth around the joey and tied two corners in a loose knot, hoping the animal would not run without him.

"You've wasted enough time," Ian said. "Give it here."

The trainer was shorter than most men who came to the Woodrat Club. Leaner than most men at the Woodrat too. The others puffed out around their chins, above their waists—bloat from too many mugs on too many nights. But there was a tightness to Ian. The scars and burns that ran across his skin described a fear-some kind of experience.

Luc shook his head no. People trudging past the alley formed a wall at his back.

Ian tipped his head to Luc to say he

understood. He reached for the handle of his hunting knife, folding his fingers around it, then let the handle go.

"Most days I'd finish this real fast," Ian said. "But I think I can teach you something."

He approached Luc like a crab, feet dancing from side to side. Luc swung first, too high, and Ian hammered his leg.

Luc was on his knees.

"Tall fella," Ian said. "I've fought tall fellas before."

Luc tried to rise up, and Ian struck his leg again.

"Thing is, most of you get to thinking that size is all you need. You never really learn how to fight."

He hurled a knee into Luc's chin, and Luc stumbled backward. He felt Ian's elbow strike the side of his head.

"Your boxing club—those matches—you lot make a game out of it," Ian said between blows. "And if you've only fought for sport? You haven't fought."

Luc swung both hands like a club, and Ian

hopped back a step to dodge them. A trickle of blood reached Luc's eye, and he charged, half blind, and fell over. Ian began to work on his ankles.

Luc spat and groaned as Ian continued to talk. "I'm doing you a favor, mate. Remember that. The other way's the knife."

Through his blurred vision, Luc saw the kangaroo, still wrapped up in a bedsheet. He pushed off of the alley ground, shoving Ian against a wall with a stiff kick. The trainer croaked and wiped some spittle from his mouth. As Luc wound up for a haymaker, Ian leapt and grabbed Luc's fist, using Luc's own weight to bring him back down.

Everything in Luc's view seemed to lose its shape as Ian yanked his arm back, the whole of the alleyway bleeding together. A stinging heat spread over the joint at Luc's shoulder while Ian pulled the arm harder and harder.

"Stop!" Luc said. "Stop . . ."

Ian released the arm and then patted Luc on the swollen joint. "There we are."

Luc lay still in the alley as Ian lifted up the kangaroo and made his way to find Mr. Hardt. Every movement revealed a new ache. Luc cursed himself for seeking mercy and wondered if he might have died otherwise. By the time he had hobbled, empty-handed, out into the street again, the blood on his face was dry, almost crumbly, and dark bruises had begun to show.

Luc spent much of that night sitting in the dark in Mrs. Maxwell's laundry room. He did not want to pass Mr. Chilton's quarters on the way toward his own. He did not want to stay in the flophouse at all, but Mr. Chilton held Luc's earnings, and Luc didn't know where else to go. With the kangaroo, it had been easy to run. Luc had known that they had to get away. Alone, he could think of nothing to do but sit.

Sometime late into the evening, Mr. Chilton stepped into the laundry space with slices of roast from that night's supper. He gave the plate to Luc and told him to eat up—he'd be expected to fight the next week. Then he left the room.

CHAPTER TEN

The week moved slowly. Luc spent long stretches in bed. The few trips he made outside were at Mr. Chilton's request. Running errands, mostly. Chilton told Luc each time to hurry or he'd have to explain himself later, though Luc would not have lingered anywhere for long. A shared suspicion shaded each exchange between the two of them.

Most of Mr. Chilton's attention went toward Mr. Hardt anyway. Hardt had not cut Chilton out of his plans after the kangaroo theft, not completely. Luc wondered if Mr. Hardt knew fewer rich men than he had claimed to know. He could hear Hardt and Chilton talking in the halls sometimes, talk he usually did not understand. But he didn't believe Mr. Chilton would end up someplace much finer than the flophouse anymore.

And yet Luc stayed. He felt tied to many things. Tied to the kangaroo, although he was afraid to go near it and risk another thrashing from Ian. Even tied to Mr. Chilton, in spite of it all.

The rush of the Bowery calmed Luc. He wouldn't step outside unless he had to, but he'd listen to the sounds from his window. Even in Quebec, Luc and the men had moved from place to place. It was nothing like Manhattan—nothing there like the street life that had become so familiar to him. And Mr. Chilton was the man who had brought Luc to the island.

As the sun went down and the streets grew quieter, Luc would try to listen for the sounds of the joey. The animal's cage was kept against the wall of another side of the flophouse, outside another row of rooms, and Luc was no more likely to hear the yawns of those rooms' tenants. Even so, he tried, with much concentration.

Few of Mr. Hardt's talks with Mr. Chilton concerned the kangaroo. The animal was back with Hardt, and it was still not yet old enough to fight, so it seemed to have hopped quickly to the back of the man's mind.

The longest mention of the animal that Luc had heard related mostly to the repairing of its cage. After bemoaning the sale of Genghis's cage, the spare, Hardt had found a shipbuilder at the Woodrat who'd been able to do the job. But the scoundrel kept trying to sell Mr. Hardt on one extra fix and then another! By the time the shipbuilder advised that Hardt get a new lock, Hardt said he might as well buy a new cage entirely, the way the builder was trying to line his pockets, and he dismissed the man. Mr. Chilton was sure the first round of repairs would be enough to keep the creature where it was, now that Luc had been disciplined.

A knock sounded at Luc's door, Mr. Chilton's musical *toc-toc-toc*.

"Luc? Are you in there, my boy?"

Chilton entered wearing a smile that Luc had not seen for more than a week.

"It's the end of your doldrums tonight, Luc, the perfect cure!" Chilton said. "I hope you've remembered you've got a match this evening." He prodded at Luc until Luc sat up in bed. "Come on, now, come on! I've even arranged a fighterly feast!"

Once seated in the dining quarters, Luc stared down at the London broil that Chilton had slid in front of him. Luc could have hidden the knotty clump of meat inside a closed fist, and he might have if Mr. Chilton hadn't been staring at him so intently. Chilton's eyes invited Luc to eat up, as if the thought of gloom dragging down Luc on a fight night was more than Chilton could bear. After all, there was money involved. Bits of gristle swam in a brown pool around Luc's food.

"We've got another twosome to contend with tonight, Luc, so you'll need your wits about you at all times. A pair of brothers up from Baltimore, I hear. Wharf trash, no doubt. You'll have to be twice as careful as with our friend Killpatrick!"

At Killpatrick's name, Luc thought of Genghis. Then, as he pushed slices of the broil across his plate, he began to think of his own face after the fight in the alleyway with Ian. Raw and pink and hot to the touch. For the first time, Luc had turned the mirror by the sink away as he'd tried to clean the wounds. One week ago. Spots of purple still covered his face like storm clouds.

Lew Mayflower muttered Mr. Chilton's name in response to Chilton's lively "Good evening." He looked up to see Luc's battered face and lost control of his cigar.

"Never you mind, Lew," Chilton said quickly. "The life of a fighter, you know . . ."

"No disrespect to the boy, but whatever did that, we'll take three of 'em," said Mayflower.

Chilton's reply was overlong, and cheers from around the club drowned out his punch line. Killpatrick stepped out of the circle, pounding a set of bloodied knuckles against his pale chest. Behind him, Oakley directed Silas and a couple of the regulars to drag Killpatrick's opponent out of sight.

One the other side of the circle, two strangers glared at Luc and Mr. Chilton. Lean, fit-looking, not much older than Luc. Brothers, maybe.

The shouts for Killpatrick had turned to woozy murmurings throughout the bar, but the men turned silent as Oakley called out the next fight.

"Williams and Williams—you're up! Chilton—get the giant ready!"

CHAPTER ELEVEN

Luc had boxed two men at once before. Often, in fact—Mr. Mayflower said the bouts drew big bets from the Woodrat's gambling types. But the Williams brothers were the first to fight like a duo. One would step forward as the other stepped back, the slightly different sounds of the brothers' grunts resembling the tick and tock of a clock. They didn't tire out so quickly this way—many men would throw jab after jab at Luc and then be spent.

Luc wondered how long it might take for the brothers to give out. He blocked some punches while others connected. A swipe across Luc's chin from one Williamses nudged a tooth loose, unless it had been Ian that loosened it. At moments like this, when Luc was distracted, the other Williams would hammer at his torso.

"Let's see some pride, Luc!" Mr. Chilton shouted.

Luc swung a fist out and threw an elbow back, not striking Williams or Williams, but clearing a few feet of space. The fight carried on this way for five minutes, maybe ten.

As Luc took another blow to the ribs but failed to stumble or fall, a chain of boos began to fill the Woodrat Club. One man flung a handful of peanut shells into the circle, then scrambled away once Oakley noticed.

"Chilton!" Lew Mayflower called out. "What's the matter with your boy? These men are getting restless, and we have more fights tonight."

"Apologies, Lew, apologies," Chilton said. "Luc! Enough pussyfooting!"

The Williams brothers, startled by the jeers from the crowd, sped up their attack. They hit Luc in tandem, hoping to force him down. Luc raised his forearms, protecting his face while his sides absorbed the brothers' knuckles. Half-formed thoughts floated through his head.

The kangaroo.

Ian's burns and scars.

The smells of the club—sweat and blood and spilled beer. So much human muck that men's boots stuck to the floor.

The kangaroo would grow up and live its life in places like this until it died.

Ian had said that if you've only fought for sport, you haven't fought. Luc had not known what the trainer meant. He hadn't even let himself think it over. But as boos throughout the club got louder, Luc decided the words were true.

The bout with Williams and Williams, every bout at the Woodrat before that—these were nothing to Luc. Luc's fight was elsewhere.

"Confound it, Luc!" Chilton shouted. "This is the most sluggish performance I've ever seen.

Tonight is the last time I prepare you a London broil, I can assure you . . ."

Luc decided that was true too.

He roared and pushed the brothers away. When they charged him again, he reached down and smacked their heads together. Both men dropped limply to the floor.

Oakley turned to Mr. Mayflower, who shrugged and lit another cigar. The bell rang as Mr. Chilton ran to Luc.

"I think my heart nearly gave out, thank you very much!" Chilton said. He cut the club's dank air with swings of his hat. "My word, Luc . . . Next time, let's see you do that at the beginning of the match! All right?"

Luc turned away from Chilton as Chilton continued to yell. A couple of men near the fighter's circle scattered when Luc lifted the wooden tabletop up from around them.

An empty barrel had held the tabletop steady. A sweet trace of bourbon filled Luc's nose for a moment and then merged with the smells of blood and salt. Luc turned back to Mr. Chilton, grabbed him by the shoulders, and stuffed him neatly inside the barrel.

Men across the Woodrat Club began to hoot and holler. Chilton's face turned red, and he shouted profane threats, but Luc was already leaving. The drunk who had thrown peanut shells tipped the barrel over and started pushing it along the ground.

One man did not laugh. Killpatrick. He stood by the doorway as Luc approached it.

The Irishman had not washed the blood off his hands since his fight earlier that evening. His eyes were pink and misty. As Luc reached the exit, Killpatrick squared his shoulders and made bricks of his fists.

But he did not throw a punch.

Luc met Killpatrick's stare and held it. Since the night they fought, Luc had been beaten down. He had felt scared, too, the way Killpatrick no doubt did. If he could have explained this to the Irishman, he would have. But he had to find his friend.

Killpatrick held his arms at his sides, but his fists began to shake. Luc's eyes met the man's anger with a simple kind of certainty. He was going to walk through the doorway. Luc knew it, and now so did the Irishman.

As Luc nudged the door open, Killpatrick did not stop him. In the days that followed, men at the Woodrat would once again whisper about Killpatrick—that his temper had been dulled, although no one would be quite sure how.

Outside, the sky was dark and a chill had set in, unfit for the summertime. Luc took his first step toward the flophouse.

CHAPTER TWELVE

Luc did not have to make many choices while he stuffed his rucksack. He grabbed a spare shirt and his other pair of pants and it was nearly full, with little left over. He left his winter coat lying on his mattress. Luc thought this would be a fair trade for the bedsheet, which he'd use in cradling the kangaroo—it had worked before.

Before leaving the room, Luc pushed his head out the window and sniffed the night air. Maybe someday he'd come back to this place.

When he reached Mr. Chilton's quarters, he was careful to turn the door handle very slowly. Locked. Luc bent over to see if light was creeping into the hallway from the rooms to the right or to the left of Mr. Chilton's. Perhaps those rooms were empty. Luc booted Chilton's door open, leaving a chunk of wood dangling at the side, locked in place.

He tried three of Chilton's hiding spots before shoving his hand into a slit in the mattress. This is how he stood when Molly Maxwell appeared in the doorway.

The toll of a Woodrat fight seemed to surprise Molly every time, and Luc waved his free hand in front of the new bruises.

"You won't find anything in there," Molly said. "He's clean out these last few days."

Luc released the mattress but stayed silent. Molly avoided his face while she spoke.

"You leaving, Luc? Looks it."

He nodded.

"Here."

She drew a small canvas bag from a pocket in her apron. Inside was an arrangement of bills and coins. She took Luc's hand—he neither pulled it back nor held it forward—and set the money in Luc's palm.

"Don't be shy about taking them, neither. Mostly from lickfingers like Chilton anyway." Molly met Luc's confused eyes and smiled. "I do more around here than fetch ice, you know. Got to keep myself occupied."

He left a couple of coins atop Mr. Chilton's bed. After Molly raised an eyebrow, Luc pointed to the ruined door and shrugged.

"Well," Molly said, "fair enough." She squeezed Luc's palm and wished him luck.

———

As Luc ducked into Mrs. Maxwell's kitchen, he heard Mr. Hardt's voice coming from the front entrance. Talking to Ian. Something about a rigged card game, though Luc couldn't make out who had done the rigging. He stayed very still until the voice traveled up the flophouse stairs and into Hardt's room.

They were in the building, Luc thought, but they were away from the cage.

He moved through the darkened laundry room and out the building's side exit, running one hand along the walls in a silent goodbye to the place. Soon he was standing before the joey, iron bars in between them. The animal purred in Luc's direction.

The bars that Luc pulled away one week earlier had been hammered straight again. Near the top of the cage, puffs of metal marked where Mr. Hardt's shipbuilder had sealed the bars back in place. At Luc's first pull, nothing happened. No metallic groan to let him know the bars were moving.

He tried again. The bars stayed put. He began to feel his ribs moan where the Williams brothers had hit him. The fight had drained Luc more than he'd realized.

He pulled at the bars yet again until a pinching at his shoulder told him to stop. He bent over, panting, while the kangaroo moved on all fours toward the front of the cage and sniffed around curiously.

Luc set down his rucksack. He had to leave that night. If there was any chance that he and Mr. Chilton might stay partners, Luc had smashed it when he kicked down the door. And he couldn't leave without the joey.

He pounded his fists against the cobblestone ground and groaned in frustration.

He would have to try another way.

The cage bars were rustiest at back—the bars that stood against the flophouse wall. Out of reach. Luc couldn't even fit a hand through the side bars to get at them. He slid a palm along his lumpy cheek.

Several men must have moved the cage for Mr. Hardt, wheeled it to the flophouse on some wagon. That night, Luc would have to be enough.

Luc set himself once more at the front of the cage. He gripped the front bars near the top, not to pry them off this time, but to pull them toward him. And with them, the rest of the cage.

Inside, the kangaroo whimpered as its pen started to shake and tilt. Luc grunted. He'd risk an arm popping out of its socket if his strength gave out too quickly.

And then the cage leaned more sharply forward, its weight lugging it toward the ground. Luc pushed against the cage suddenly, holding it steady long enough to step out from underneath. Then its front side clattered against the alley's cobblestones.

Luc's ears rang from the crash. The kangaroo twitched in fear. The cage's iron lid stood ajar, split off from some of the back bars by the force of the collision. With a final grunt, Luc pried the top away.

The joey crawled shyly toward him. A moment later, someone from inside the flophouse moaned, "What the devil is all that noise!?"

Mr. Hardt stuck his head out of a window two stories above, a long nightcap crowning his matted hair.

"Listen here, you shut—you. You ape!" Hardt shouted. "You mongrel! Thief! Thief! Anyone—stop him! Thief!"

Hardt yanked his head back and started yelling for Ian. One window over, Ian threw back his curtain. He appeared in silhouette for a moment in the dark of his room, then vanished. Already heading down the stairs.

Luc laid the bedsheet out before the kangaroo. It was time they left the Bowery.

CHAPTER THIRTEEN

Once Luc crossed Houston Street, he stopped looking back. Block after block, he hurtled through lower Manhattan.

The commotion on the streets had slowed after nightfall but hadn't stopped—person after person stared unbelieving at the figure running past them, first because of the boy's height and then because of the bundle he carried. The joey had nipped at Luc's arms at first, but it relaxed as he settled into a rhythm, each stride landing with a predictable thump.

Luc was too big to hide in Manhattan. He was one of the few who couldn't shield himself in its crowds. As he neared Fulton Street, no other choices came to mind: they had to go to the water.

The smells of the fish market told Luc he was near. Most fishmongers had left the seaport hours earlier, but hints of bass and flounder clung to the tents and tables. Luc and the kangaroo stopped at South Street, the East River stretched out before them.

If Luc was too large to sneak through the city, then he was too large to sneak aboard a boat. He pictured a scrum of sailors shoving him overboard, the boat rocking, the joey kept for lunch. He would not do much better if he had to barter his way onto a ship, but maybe some captain needed strong hands. If the man spoke French, all the better. Possibilities at both extremes ran through Luc's head.

He sat against a stack of crates for a moment as his heart slowed to its usual speed. Sat and ached.

Boats of many sizes lined the seaport. Luc looked from one to another, his intuition failing him. Which crew might help? How would he even ask? Some of the men along the dock squinted at Luc's hulking outline as they smoked tobacco or dumped old chum into the water.

The distant chatter of these men merged with the sound of the river currents and occasional honks from the larger ships. And then Luc heard a foreign clopping above the seaport noise. Hooves against the ground, getting louder.

He wrestled the lid off one of the crates behind him and set the joey inside. As blood rushed to his head, he watched Ian the trainer speed closer. The man raced on horseback down the South Street boardwalk.

Soon Ian was close enough for Luc to see the man's pearly black eyes. The trainer tied the horse's reins to a fish stand, quickly and neatly.

"Luc," he said. "That's your name, yeah? Luc—I'd rather be inside resting than out here chasing thieves. I hate the smell of fish. And the owner of this horse's going to notice pretty soon that his animal went missing. Forget all that—mate, we've done this before. I can still see your bruises, even. So give me the kangaroo."

Luc breathed in and said, "No."

Ian drew his hunting knife. "I'll kill ya this time. Understand?"

Luc decided the trainer would have to.

Ian began his crablike walk, knife in hand. Luc tried to watch Ian's shoulders, to guess where the man might lunge, but he couldn't keep his eyes from the blade. Every movement of Ian's was fast but controlled—no wild swipes. Luc wanted to keep his footing, but step by step he moved backward, edging away from the tip of the knife.

With a flick of his wrist, Ian sliced through the front of Luc's shirt, missing Luc's white belly by a hair. Luc cried in alarm and thrust a boot forward, knocking Ian in the chest and sending him toward the ground. Ian landed on the ground as if he had arranged the fall himself—his body snapped into a roll. He looked up at Luc, wiping his mouth with the back of his free hand.

The man's actions were different from anything he had known. But Luc was different too. He was ready for the fight Ian had talked about.

Ian thrust the knife forward and pulled it back again. When he did, Luc dove at the man's waist, bringing them both onto the ground.

Ian's arm twisted and trembled as he tried to lift his blade. Luc closed his hand around Ian's wrist. He held it firm against the ground.

Ian tucked his knees, then kicked at Luc's chin, his throat. Luc roared and shifted his weight, but not before slamming Ian's arm against the boardwalk. The trainer's knife spun onto the boards. Luc tripped over himself trying to grab it.

Both fighters scrambled to pick up the weapon. Luc's long arm reached it first—he tossed the knife blindly through the air and heard a comforting *plup*. Into the river.

The boards where Luc had tackled Ian were dented, and a piece of splintered wood snagged his foot as he charged the trainer. Stumbling, Luc swung at Ian with an open palm. Ian caught Luc's hand in both of his, then drove his shin into Luc's face.

Another kick, then another, hammering at Luc's arms and chest. Luc gasped and tried to breathe and couldn't. Staggering away from the trainer, he backed onto the damaged boards. Only after the wood began to creak did Luc understand the danger.

Luc watched Ian blur and disappear. Then he saw only black. The river was cold, and it began to fill Luc's nose and mouth before he realized he'd fallen in.

CHAPTER FOURTEEN

Luc's head found the surface, and he coughed and spat. He couldn't swim, had never learned. His head fell under again. He was blind—not even moonlight reached underneath the boardwalk.

Luc thrashed about in the water as if anchored to the deep. He would find the air again only to lose it. With every push, he moved closer to shore or father away, couldn't tell. More water filled his mouth.

His mind rushed to the kangaroo and to Molly Maxwell and to Mr. Chilton. He stomped at the river with his heavy boots, not letting himself stay under. And when he collided with a wooden pillar below the boards, he held on with a force that threatened to splinter his only salvation.

Both arms wrapped around the pillar, Luc pulled himself above the river's surface. He clung to the wood for a moment, dripping wet, and shuddered. Then he continued to climb, inching up until he laid a hand on the boardwalk above.

Ian had untethered his horse and led it toward the crate that held the kangaroo. Luc's pounding footsteps preceded him; he appeared to Ian like a black mountaintop, backlit by the yellow moon.

"Mother of . . . ," Ian said. "You're not makin' this one easy, are you?"

The trainer squatted and sent a foot toward Luc's knee, grazing it, enough to cut Luc down. The horse neighed in panic and took off running.

Luc clasped his hands together and lobbed them against Ian, too much force for the trainer to block. Ian snapped up again with a chop to Luc's throat. Luc grabbed the trainer's hand, as he had with Killpatrick. His fist became a bear trap of his own.

Luc held his arm out, far enough that the man couldn't connect with another kick. Thinking again of the kangaroo, he pressed Ian's hand until bones began to crumple.

Ian hissed, starting to form a string of words and abandoning it.

Luc held steady while the trainer appeared to contract. Ian crouched down, writhing, and then—a glint in the moonlight.

The man yanked a dagger from his boot, his free hand swishing the blade. He raised his arm, howling at Luc, and then collapsed onto the seaport.

Luc hobbled away from the trainer's silent, limp body. The joey was still safe in its crate. If the fighting outside had disturbed the animal, Luc couldn't make out how. The joey purred as Luc wrapped it back into the bedsheet.

Some men had run from the boardwalk as soon as the ruckus started. Maybe men who had reason to hide if the police came by, Luc thought. Some of the others had kept their distance but stayed, staring. Luc's legs were weak, and he approached the one who meant the least amount of walking.

From the crates, the man had looked like a stout blue chimney, clouds of smoke hiding his face. Up close, Luc made out a gray beard and a navy-colored sweater.

The man reeled back and rubbed his eyes. He blinked and squinted as if trying to bring Luc into focus. "Good God almighty, I thought I was havin' one of my gin visions again. You look like a barge hit you, son." He chuckled, then pointed to the kangaroo. "I like your dog."

"Thank you," Luc said.

"Scrawny little fella."

Luc smiled.

"So what brings a brob-dinger like you out to the river this late? You fixin' for a lift someplace?"

Luc nodded.

The sailor puffed on his pipe. "Well, we're departin' for Providence in a few hours. Couple stops on the way there. Hadn't expected extra cargo, let alone something your size...What do you think, son, can you lift a tuna net? Heard talk about a whole swarm of bluefins nearer to Rhode Island. I reckon we can take you that far, anyway."

The other fishermen were suspicious when Luc stepped on board. They looked older, most of them, like the sailor in the navy sweater. They had the eyes of people who had cheated or been cheated many times in their lives and took nothing for granted.

Luc's weight rocked the boat awkwardly. In his tiredness, he overcorrected, sending it the other way. The sailor in the navy sweater told him to sit down or be knocked down, that when they needed a new mast he'd ask outright. The others laughed and seemed pleased when Luc laughed too.

After Luc fed the joey some bread crusts, Luc's eyes began to close. He tried to fight the

fatigue, but it was no use. The blue sailor promised to wake him further into the morning, in
time to drag up the haul. Luc drifted asleep beneath the bleary sight of daybreak.

CHAPTER FIFTEEN

The man in the top hat spoke with practiced excitement, yanking his lapel for emphasis at the end of every line: "We're about to show you something very special now, ladies and gentlemen. Are you ready to be amazed? Are you ready to witness feats of strength the likes of which you've never seen? Here, for this evening only, and hailing from the Great White North, a towering titan of unbeeelievable power... Luc the Indomitable!"

As the cheers of the crowd rushed behind the striped curtain, a gaggle of men in white face paint began a winding walk into the center of the tent. A few held each side of the barbell above the ground as they went. Luc followed them out, to fresh applause. The clowns dropped the weight in unison and collapsed onto the dirt.

Luc stepped up to the barbell, waved at the people in the stands, and then lifted the weight cleanly above his head. The clowns jumped up as if caught napping once Luc let it hit the ground.

"Luc, ladies and gentleman!" the ringmaster shouted. For an encore, he asked if anyone had brought heavy cargo along from home.

Later that night, as the show came to a close, Luc made his way out of the tent, toward the circus caravan. Gerhard the contortionist called hello from underneath the head wagon. This surprised Luc every time.

Thick fields stretched out in most directions,

looking at sundown like bands of gold. Iowa was a nice place, Luc decided. Next week he would see Minnesota.

Past the last of the wagons, Luc found the animal pens and took out his key. With a grin, he unlocked the kangaroo's cage.

The kangaroo had grown quickly in the months since they'd left New York, although Luc was still much taller. The move had been a good one, even if it started rough. Everyone on the caravan was very kind to the animal. Luc made sure of that. As he held out his sack of grass and shrubs, the kangaroo moved toward him on all fours.

Luc patted the animal on the neck and then opened the sack wide, letting the kangaroo nuzzle its way inside. He'd been worried at first when the animal's gray fur began to grow coarser, but P. W., who trained the monkeys, said that this was just what happened. They grew up that way.

Luc laughed as the bag shook around in his hands. When the kangaroo finished eating, he patted it one last time. It lay down on its side, content, as Luc closed the cage again. He locked the door slowly so the animal could drift off without interruption.

"Dors bien, mon ami," Luc said—Sleep well, my friend.

About the Author

Jonathan Mary-Todd is a dream weaver from the Twin Cities.

BARE KNUCKLE

WELCOME TO THE DOJO

LEARN TO FIGHT, LEARN TO LIVE, AND LEARN TO FIGHT FOR YOUR LIFE.

BODY SHOT
PATRICK JONES

HEAD KICK
PATRICK JONES

SIDE CONTROL
PATRICK JONES

TRIANGLE CHOKE
PATRICK JONES

AFTER THE DUST SETTLED

AFTER THE DUST SETTLED

PLAGUE RIDERS

GABRIEL GOODMAN

AFTER THE DUST SETTLED

FIGHT THE WIND

CLARA CARR

AFTER THE DUST SETTLED

RIVER RUN

DOMENIC BLACK

AFTER THE DUST SETTLED

PIG CITY

JONATHAN MARY-TODD

AFTER THE DUST SETTLED

SHOT DOWN

JONATHAN MARY-TODD

AFTER THE DUST SETTLED

SNAKEBITE

JONATHAN MARY-TODD

The world is over.
Can you survive what's next?